This book is a work of fiction. Any references to historical events, real people, or real places are used fictitiously. Other names, characters, places, and events are products of the author's imagination, and any resemblance to actual events or places or persons, living or dead, is entirely coincidental.

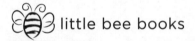

An imprint of Bonnier Publishing USA
251 Park Avenue South, New York, NY 10010
Copyright © 2018 by Little Bee Books
All rights reserved, including the right of reproduction in whole or in part in any form.
Little Bee Books is a trademark of Bonnier Publishing USA, and associated colophon is a trademark of Bonnier Publishing USA.
Library of Congress Cataloging-in-Publication Data is available upon request.
Printed in the United States of America LAK 0918
ISBN 978-1-4998-0760-8 (hc)
First Edition 10 9 8 7 6 5 4 3 2 1
ISBN 978-1-4998-0759-2 (pb)
First Edition 10 9 8 7 6 5 4 3 2 1
littlebeebooks.com
bonnierpublishingusa.com

THE MAJOR EIGHTS

THE NEW BANDMATE

by Melody Reed
illustrated by Émilie Pépin

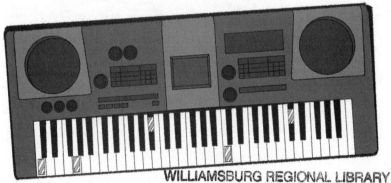

little bee books

CONTENTS

"In third place is . . . Jasmine Li!"

I blinked. Had he just said my name?

Sure enough, the judge in charge of the piano competition waved me up onstage. Three trophies sat on the table behind him. He handed me the shortest one.

"Thanks," I murmured, trying to smile. I'd practiced every day for a month. I really thought I had a shot at first place this time. Oh, well. At least I'd won *something*.

"And in second place is . . . Nate Stevens!"

A boy rushed up from the back of the room. His family cheered for him.

Becca, Maggie, and Scarlet smiled at me from the front row. My parents and my brother, Nick, sat behind them. It was a Saturday. The room at the community center was packed. The regional competition is a big deal every year.

The judge gave Nate his trophy, then picked up the last one. The *biggest* one. "And finally, first place goes to . . . Leslie Miller!"

Leslie's red pigtails bounced as she skipped up the steps. She shook the judge's free hand. Her grin stretched from ear to ear. The trophy was so big, she had to hold it with both of her hands.

Leslie had won another piano competition.

But I forced myself to smile anyway. "Good job," I told her.

"You, too!" Leslie beamed. "Your piece was nice."

I smiled for real. Staying mad at Leslie for long was hard to do.

Becca put a hand on my shoulder. "I'm sorry, Jas," she said. "I know you worked hard for this."

"Really good job," said Scarlet. Maggie nodded next to her.

"Thanks, guys." I smiled at my friends.

"See you tomorrow for practice?" Maggie asked.

I grinned. "That's right! We have the show at Tony's next week." Tony's Tacos is a restaurant downtown. Tony, the owner, had heard our band play and asked us to perform a song for his customers sometime. "I'll see you guys tomorrow!"

"Good job, honey," said my mom.

"Proud of you, Jasmine," said my dad.

"Hey, Jas," said Nick. "Next time, maybe you should wear pigtails."

I frowned. "Ha-ha."

"No, I'm serious," he said. "Leslie keeps winning competitions and you don't. Either she has magic hair or she's just better at piano than you."

"Nick," warned my dad, "I believe that's enough."

8

I balled up my fists. "She is *not* better than me!"

My parents scooted us all out of the building. Some of the kids from the competition were horsing around on the community center playground.

Leslie hung from the high bar. "Jasmine," she called. "Come play with us!"

I zipped over to the playground and pulled up on the bar next to Leslie.

"Watch how far I can go!" she said. She swung off the bar and let go, landing on her feet.

"I bet I can go farther," I said. I swung my body to pick up speed.

But just as I was about to let go, one of my hands slipped. I crashed to the ground.

A sharp pain ran up my arm.

Leslie ran over. "Oh, no! Jasmine, are you okay?"

I sat up. My arm hurt so much I couldn't think straight. I tried to move my fingers, but I couldn't. "No," I gasped. "I don't think so!"

2

MY BIG BREAK

I sat on the exam table, my arm still throbbing. Mom stood next to me, holding the hand that didn't hurt. Dad and Nick sat across from us. As soon as I'd fallen, Mom had hurried us into the car. We'd driven straight to Scarlet's dad's office, as he's a doctor.

I'd never seen Scarlet's dad at work before. Instead of the jeans and funny T-shirt he usually had on, he wore a white lab coat. I squinted at his name badge. "Or-tho-pah-"

Dr. Johnson smiled at me. "Orthopedic surgeon."

I frowned. "Scarlet said you were a bone doctor."

"An orthopedic doctor *is* a bone doctor," said Dr. Johnson. "I specialize in the human skeleton."

"Oh."

Dr. Johnson stared at my X-ray on the screen with a bright light behind it. It was mostly gray, but there was an outline of an arm—*my* arm. If I'd felt better, I probably would've thought it was cool. "Well, I hate to break it to you," he said, "but it's broken."

"No," I groaned.

"Get it, Jas?" Nick elbowed me. "Hate to *break* it to you?"

I scowled at Nick.

Dr. Johnson pointed to a tiny line in the X-ray. It was all crooked, like the edge of a broken eggshell. "Look," he said. "This is where the fracture is."

Mom frowned. "Will she need a cast?"

"Yes. She'll need to wear a cast for three weeks while the bone heals."

My eyes bugged. "Three weeks?!" I turned to Mom. "We have the show at Tony's next week. I can't play the keyboard in a cast!"

Dr. Johnson frowned. "I'm sorry, Jasmine."

"Guess you'll have to . . . take a *break*," Nick said with a chuckle.

I glared at him. "Not funny."

Mom shook her head. "I'm sorry, honey. The band will have to perform without you."

The Major Eights couldn't play without me. The band had been my idea to begin with.

Becca, Maggie, and Scarlet wouldn't do that.

Would they?

THE BAD NEWS

I slouched in front of my keyboard. The basement was quiet. At any moment now, the other Major Eights would be here for practice. I hadn't told any of them yet.

My left arm was in a cast—a hot pink one, which Dr. Johnson had let me pick. Like that would cheer me up.

I could wiggle my fingers and thumb a little bit. Maybe I could still play with my cast.

Spreading my fingers out, I pressed a few keys.

Ugh. It sounded awful! The cast had gotten in the way.

Just then, Maggie bounced down the stairs, followed by Scarlet. "Hey, Jasmine!" they said.

Becca came down last. "Jasmine, your mom said you had something to tell all of us."

I took a deep breath and lifted up my arm, revealing my cast.

My friends gasped.

"What *happened*?" asked Scarlet.

"I fell on the playground after the piano competition," I told them. But I didn't tell them how I'd tried to beat Leslie at piano *and* at swinging off the bar. Leslie was probably better than me at just about everything.

"Does it hurt?" asked Maggie.

I shrugged. "Not anymore. But it hurt a lot when I broke it."

"It's okay, Jas," Becca said. "My brothers break bones almost every year. I broke my wrist when I was five. Things like that happen all the time."

"Hold on." Scarlet's eyes got big. "Our show at Tony's! What are we going to do?"

I shook my head sadly. "I guess we'll have to tell Tony we can't play anymore."

Becca frowned. "But we can't back out now!"

"Yeah," Maggie said. "And this is the first time we're being paid—all the tacos we can eat!"

"I guess we could play . . . without a keyboard," suggested Becca.

Scarlet frowned. "But we don't sound as good without the keyboard."

Becca paced back and forth. Then she turned to face us. "I have an idea. Our keyboard player broke her arm, but"—she added with a grin—"we know somebody else who can play."

I frowned.

"Who?" asked Maggie.

Becca put her hands on her hips. "Leslie!"

"That's a *great* idea!" Scarlet shouted.

"Yeah!" said Maggie.

I blinked. Was this for real?

"I mean, it's perfect, right?" said Becca. "She's great at piano."

"And Leslie is so nice, too!" said Maggie. "I bet she would say yes."

"Hey, what do you think, Jas?" asked Scarlet.

I tried to cross my arms, but my cast was too big. *I* had started this band. And now they wanted to play without me. And not just without me—they wanted to play with Leslie. Leslie who was better at piano than me. What if she was better *in the band*, too?

But my friends looked so hopeful. I didn't want to let Becca, Maggie, and Scarlet down.

I swallowed the lump in my throat. "Well . . . I guess so."

Becca hugged Scarlet and Maggie, but I stayed in my seat.

I wished I could take the cast off. I also wished I didn't need it.

But then I remembered Leslie wasn't in the band yet. Maybe she wouldn't want to be. She was always busy. Maybe, just *maybe*, she'd say no to joining.

THE NEWEST MAJOR EiGHT

The bell rang for recess the next day, and kids ran onto the blacktop outside. I dodged a ball flying toward me. I ducked away from a jump rope. Finally, I made it to the swing set. The Major Eights were already there waiting for me.

"Is Leslie coming?" Becca asked.

My shoulders fell. "Yeah, she'll be over in a bit."

I'd asked Leslie that morning to meet us here at recess, but I hadn't told her why.

Leslie bounced over to us. Her pigtails swung behind her, and she had a big smile on her face. "Hi, guys," she said. "What's going on?"

"Hi, Leslie," said Maggie. "Thanks for coming."

"We need your help," Scarlet said.

"Jasmine broke her arm, and she can't play keyboard anymore and—"

"Just for three weeks," I interrupted.

"—and we have a show next week," Scarlet finished.

"We'd really love it if you'd sub in for her," said Becca.

"Just for this one show," I added. But in my head, I thought, *Please say no, please say no!*

Leslie's eyes got as big as dodge balls. "Really?!" she squealed. "You want *me* to join the Major Eights?!" She jumped up and down, her pigtails dancing.

I frowned. "Just for this one show," I said again, a little louder this time.

Becca grinned. "Does that mean you'll do it?"

"YES!" shouted Leslie. "I've always wanted to be part of a band!"

I frowned. "But Leslie, what about the next piano competition? You won't have as much time to practice. Are you sure you want to do this?"

Becca elbowed me.

"Well . . . yes!" said Leslie. "I don't have another one for a while."

"Awesome!" Becca yelled.

"Fantastic!" Maggie shouted.

"Super!" Scarlet cheered.

I kicked at the dirt. "Uh, great," I mumbled.

THE FiRST PRACTiCE

Our first practice with Leslie was that day after school.

"Don't worry, Jasmine," Maggie said. "We still need you."

"Really?" I asked.

"Sure." Becca unzipped her gig bag. "Leslie will need help learning our material. We need you to show her what to do."

My shoulders slumped. "Oh."

37

Leslie skipped down the stairs. "Hey, guys. Am I late?"

"Right on time!" Scarlet held up my hairbrush, ready to sing into it.

"There's where you'll be." Becca pointed to the keyboard.

Leslie sprang over to it. She stood in *my* spot and put her hands on *my* keyboard. "Wow," she said. "I guess there aren't as many keys on a keyboard as there are on a piano."

"Have you ever played a keyboard before?" I asked.

She shook her head. "We only have a piano at home." She studied the keys. "What do you do when you need to play, like, a really high C? Or a really low C? Keys that aren't on the keyboard?"

I shrugged. "You play a *different* C. Like one in the middle."

"Oh."

"Okay, guys." Becca strummed her guitar. "Ready for 'In Your Dreams'?"

Scarlet struck a pose with her hairbrush mic.

Maggie hit her sticks together behind the drum set.

I crossed my arms—or tried to.

But Leslie obviously wasn't ready. She looked under the bench. She searched through some papers I'd left next to it.

"What's wrong?" Scarlet asked.

"Where's your sheet music for the song?" Leslie whispered to me.

"Oh, right." I pulled the song out of the stack by the bench. "Here you go. This should help."

Leslie frowned at the paper. "But, these are just letters. Where are the notes?"

"The letters are the chords," I explained. "I don't use sheet music for this song."

"Sorry, Leslie," Maggie piped up. "I guess we should've let you practice on your own first."

I rolled my eyes. "You know, *chords*." I leaned over Leslie and played three keys at the same time with my good hand. "Or you can break them up." I played the three keys one at a time.

Leslie swallowed. "So . . . you just *make up* the keyboard part?"

"Well, yeah. Sometimes."

"Okay, I'll try." She studied the sheet, then played a chord. "The keys are stuck," she said. "No sound comes out when I press this one."

"Yeah." I shrugged. "Just don't play the keys that stick. That's what I do."

"Which ones stick?"

"This one, this one, this one"—I touched each of the broken keys—"and this one . . . oh, and this one."

Leslie's eyes got bigger with each new key I pointed to.

"You got it?" I asked.

"Um, sure. N-no problem."

"Go ahead and start," I told the band. "She'll catch up."

Hmm, I thought. *If Leslie can't keep up, maybe the band will change their minds. Maybe they won't want her to play with them after all.*

But Leslie started to get the hang of the keyboard after that. She played more and more chords on time.

Becca grinned as she strummed. "Leslie, you're doing great!"

Leslie didn't look up, but she smiled. Her pigtails swung as she moved to a new chord.

I scowled.

Leslie hit a dead key. Then she fell behind in the song.

By the end of the it, Leslie's cheeks were pink. "I'm really sorry, you guys."

"You did fine, Leslie!" Becca said. "You just need some practice."

"Yeah, all of us make mistakes," added Maggie.

"That was really good for your first try," said Scarlet.

I scratched my head. Hadn't they heard all of Leslie's mistakes?

"You think so?" Leslie asked.

"Definitely!" said Becca. "Let's play again tomorrow."

I couldn't *believe* my friends. Leslie needed sheet music. She couldn't keep up. She couldn't avoid the dead keys. She was *not* a good fit for our band at all.

Why was I the only one who could see it?

GOOD ADVICE

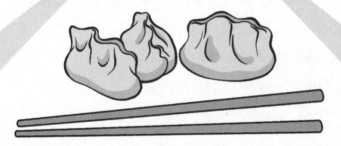

I slumped into a chair in the kitchen that night. My cast made a *clunk* sound on the table.

"I'm making your favorite," my mom said. "Dumplings."

"Thanks," I mumbled.

Mom poured herself a mug of tea. "How did it go with Leslie today?"

"Just great," I muttered sarcastically.
"Didn't the other girls like her?"

"That's the problem," I said. "They *do* like her. She made tons of mistakes, and they still like her. She's ruining the song."

Mom sipped her tea. "Your friends don't seem to think so."

I stared down at my lap. "What if they don't want me back in the band when my arm heals?"

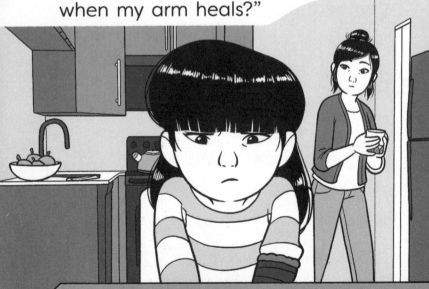

"Oh, honey." Mom put an arm around me. "Try to think about what's best for the band. Maybe you could help Leslie. Teach her what she needs to know."

I sat up straighter. I hadn't thought about it that way.

Maybe the band *did* need me. They couldn't hear Leslie's mistakes. And Leslie didn't know how to fix them. Maybe more help was what they all needed!

"You hit a dead key!" I shouted over the song the next day. The Major Eights were back in my basement. Leslie stood behind my keyboard once again.

Leslie kept playing. Maybe she didn't hear me.

"You skipped that chord," I said louder, pointing to the sheet in front of her.

Leslie paused. She missed a few more chords. She studied the sheet.

Scarlet frowned at me as she sang.

I nodded back. Leslie was falling behind. Scarlet must have noticed it, too.

"Don't forget to look at Maggie," I told Leslie to help her catch up. "Maggie's the one keeping time."

Leslie missed the next three chords. "Um, wait . . . it's okay . . . I think I've got it," she said.

The rest of the band played the last chord. Scarlet sang her last word, using lots of different notes. This was supposed to end the song. But Leslie had finally found her last chord. She played it right in the middle of Scarlet's riff.

"Leslie, you *have* to keep up," I scolded. "You played that note way too late!"

"I know, I know!" Leslie sobbed. "I'm sorry, guys, but I don't think I can be in your band."

"No, hold on a second," said Maggie. "You just need to practice with us more is all."

But Leslie shook her head. "I'm sorry, everybody. I can't do this." She ran across the floor and thundered up the stairs.

Becca unstrapped her guitar and ran after her. "Leslie, wait!"

Maggie rushed after them.

I shrugged at Scarlet. "I guess she can't handle it."

But Scarlet just frowned and ran out, too.

I was left alone in the basement.

7

THE BUMPY RIDE

The next morning, I found Becca, Maggie, and Scarlet sitting together on the bus. I sat down in the open seat next to Maggie. The sky was blue and the sun was shining. It was going to be a great day.

"Hi, guys!" I said.

But my friends frowned once they saw it was me. "What's up?" I asked.

"In case you didn't notice, our band isn't doing so good," Scarlet said.

"I know," I agreed. "Leslie's pretty bad. I guess we won't be able to do the show at Tony's."

"Leslie isn't the problem, Jasmine," Becca said. "*You* are."

I blinked. "What? But . . . Leslie can't keep a beat. She misses entire chords." I elbowed Maggie. "Right, Maggie?"

"Well, she *does* do those things. . . ."

"You're scaring her, Jasmine," Becca said. "I think you're making her mess up on purpose."

I crossed my arms. "I'm trying to help her. I'm trying to help us, the band."

"But you're not!" Becca said.

The bus pulled up at school.

"Please, Jasmine," said Scarlet as she stood up. "We *need* you."

She and Becca and Maggie got off the bus.

I sighed. I guess it wasn't going to be such a great day anymore. I walked off the bus alone.

Were my friends right?

I thought about how Leslie had been happy when we first asked her to help. But she was getting more upset at every practice. Was it because of me?

My friends said they needed me, but for what? It wasn't to play the keyboard. And maybe it wasn't to point out all of Leslie's mistakes to her, either.

There must be another way I could help the Major Eights.

Because broken arm or not, I was still their friend. And friends help each other no matter what. Which meant only one thing ... I had a show to save!

SECOND CHANCES

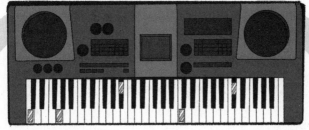

Knock, knock!

I took a deep breath and opened the door.

Leslie stood on the mat. She kept looking away, like she didn't want to be there.

I swallowed. "Thanks for coming."

She nodded, but still didn't look me in the eyes.

"I wanted to say I'm sorry," I continued, staring at my feet. "I was mad I broke my arm and couldn't play." I sighed. "But that's not your fault. I want to help you now. The band needs you," I said, finally looking at Leslie.

Leslie smiled a little. "Thanks, Jasmine. They need you, too, you know."

"Can I show you something?" I gently asked.

She nodded, sliding off her shoes.

I led her down to the basement and pointed to the keyboard. "I made some changes. My mom said I could."

Leslie blinked. "Is that Washi tape on the keys?"

I beamed. "Yup, just a few of the keys. Go ahead, play them!"

Leslie touched a key with pink-and-white striped tape on it. "Nothing's happening."

"Exactly. Try the next one."

She tried all five. Her eyes lit up. "You marked all the dead keys!"

"I thought it would be easier to keep track of them that way."

I handed her a few sheets of paper. "What's this?"

"I wrote out the music for you," I said. "So you don't have to make it up every time. I know you're used to reading music when you play."

"Thanks, Jasmine." She gave me a big hug.

"Will you still play with the band at the show?"

Leslie thought for a moment. "Yes. But maybe you could show me again how you rearrange chords? I want to learn that, too. Deal?"

I grinned back. "Deal."

TACO TIME!

The night of the show, I waited outside Tony's Tacos. A car pulled up in front and I raced over to meet it.

"Leslie!" I shouted. "The band is all set up. Are you ready?"

She chewed her lip, stepping out of the car. "I don't know, Jasmine. I've been practicing, but I still don't feel ready."

I put an arm around her as we rushed inside. "Oh, you'll do great. Don't worry."

Tony had set up a mini stage in one corner. Forks clinked on plates. People talked and laughed at their tables. It was so loud, I wanted to cover my ears.

"Hurry!" Scarlet urged. She stood at the mic stand. Becca had her guitar on and Maggie sat at the drums. The bench at the keyboard was empty.

"Thanks for coming tonight , Leslie!" Becca said.

Scarlet grinned. "We're so glad to see you!"

But Maggie frowned. "Leslie, what's wrong?"

Leslie looked out at the crowd. "I-I'm just a little nervous. Jasmine was helping me, but—"

Becca raised an eyebrow. "*Jasmine was helping you?*"

But before either Leslie or I could explain, Tony hopped up onstage. He threw us a grin and grabbed the mic.

"Hey, folks," he said. "Thank you for coming out tonight. Tony's Tacos is pleased to present a very talented local band. They dazzled us all at the Fall Festival. Please welcome . . . the Major Eights!"

Only a few people got quiet and even fewer clapped.

Tony shrugged at us. "Sorry about the noise. Do your best to play over it, I guess."

I hugged Leslie. "Break a finger," I whispered.

She glanced at me with big eyes. "What?!"

"It means good luck!" I hopped off the stage.

Leslie hurried to the bench.

I stood over in a corner to watch, which felt funny. I was used to being up onstage. But then I thought about what my mom had said. "Best for the band," I said under my breath.

Scarlet sang the first line. Becca strummed a few chords.

But most people weren't paying attention. They were still talking and eating their tacos.

The band was a few measures in. Maggie started a beat on the kick drum. Leslie was supposed to come in after that, but she didn't. Instead, she hit one of the keys, over and over again. She was frowning.

Scarlet missed the next line.

I moved closer to Leslie. "What's wrong?" I whispered.

"I can't hear the keyboard!" she said. "And it's not just the broken keys."

I peeked over Leslie's shoulder. The keyboard was correctly plugged in. That wasn't the problem. I glanced around the stage—aha! The keyboard had a power switch on top of it, but it was turned to off!

Scarlet was still a line behind. Maggie couldn't keep the beat. Leslie looked like she was about to cry.

I scurried over to the keyboard and flipped the switch. I smiled at Leslie and gave her a thumbs-up.

But Leslie shook her head and stopped playing. "The crowd is too loud, Jasmine! I can barely hear Maggie."

By now, Maggie and Scarlet had stopped, too.

Tony rushed over. "What's wrong?" he asked.

Plates clanged harder. The talking grew to a roar.

"I have an idea!" I said. "Sorry for the delay, Tony." I stepped up next to Scarlet. My idea had better work. Or everyone was going to laugh at me! Taking a deep breath, I grabbed the mic. "Who loves Tony's Tacos?" I shouted into it.

For a second, the room got quiet.

Then a guy in the back of the restaurant whooped. A kid giggled loudly up front. People set down their food for a moment and turned to face the stage.

"What are you *doing*, Jasmine?" hissed Becca.

I covered the mic. "Leslie couldn't hear the beat," I told Becca. "We need the audience's attention so they'll be quieter."

"I think you have it," Scarlet whispered. "Are you sure about this?"

"Sure," I insisted.

But I swallowed. I wasn't really sure what I was doing at all.

FOREVER A
MAJOR EiGHT

I leaned toward the mic again. "So, uh . . . what did the taco say to the sad burrito?"

The audience was quiet and my heart thumped.

"What?" a kid finally yelled.

My throat felt dry. "Do you want to taco 'bout it?"

Scarlet giggled. Maggie hit the cymbal behind me.

I had the crowd's attention.

"So, let's give it up for four more taco fans—the Major Eights!" I waved to the band and quickly hopped off the stage.

The audience clapped and then they stayed quiet!

I nodded to Scarlet to start right away before they got loud again.

Scarlet nodded. She began to sing.
Becca came in on guitar.

Maggie started a beat on the kick drum.

Leslie's chin bobbed, keeping time with the beat. She came in with the first chord.

She sounded great! I caught Leslie's eye and smiled. We almost started giggling, right there in the middle of a show.

I never thought having Leslie in the band would be so much fun.

At the end of the song, Leslie and Becca played the last chord at the same time. Scarlet finished with an amazing riff.

The audience cheered.

I rushed up to Leslie. "You did it!" I shouted.

"That was so great!" She pulled me in for a hug and almost fell off the bench. "You fixed it!"

Tony came onstage. "The Major Eights, everyone!" He waved a hand at us and stepped to the side.

The audience hollered and hooted their approval.

Scarlet, Becca, and Maggie stood next to one another to take a bow. Becca waved Leslie over to join them.

Leslie grinned, but didn't let go of my hand. "You're coming, too, Jasmine!" she said.

Becca smiled and made room for me. All five of us took a bow.

As we were leaving the stage, Becca caught up to me. "Thank you so much, Jasmine."

"Yeah—thank you," said Maggie.

I shrugged. "Sometimes you've got to do what's best for the band."

Leslie's parents came over and hugged her. "That was great, honey. Ready to eat, rock star?" asked her dad.

"Almost," she said. She turned to us. "Guys, thanks for giving me a chance to play in the band. It was really fun!" She turned to me. "And if you ever need me again, I'll be there. But now I've got to practice for the next piano competition. I signed up for another one today."

"Thanks for helping us out!" I said. "And thank you for giving me another chance."

Leslie grinned. She hugged me again and left to join her parents.

"I'm sorry we were mad at you, Jasmine," said Becca. "We know now that you were just trying to help Leslie."

I swallowed. "But I didn't help her at first. I tried to point out Leslie's mistakes. I just . . . I wanted to make sure you'd still want me in the band once my arm healed."

Scarlet wrinkled her forehead. "You were worried that we wouldn't want you back in the band?"

I nodded, looking at my feet.

Becca put an arm around me. "Remember when we said we needed you?"

"You're our *friend*, Jasmine," said Maggie. "We love making new friends, but that doesn't mean we want to lose *you*."

"And you do so much for the band," said Scarlet. "Not just playing keyboard. You make sure everything goes smoothly onstage."

"You're also the one who wanted us to start performing, remember?" said Becca. "You gave us courage then and still do now."

"Major Eights forever!" said Scarlet.

"And forever a Major Eight," said Becca, poking me.

I smiled so hard, my cheeks hurt.

Tony set five plates heaped with tacos at a nearby booth. "Your payment!" he said. "Thanks for coming, girls. You did awesome."

We piled in on top of each other for a huge hug.

It was truly a great day.

Read on for a sneak peek from the sixth book in THE MAJOR EiGHTS series, *The Secret Valentine.*

THE MAJOR EIGHTS

THE SECRET VALENTINE

BOOK 6

CASSIE

Sweat dripped down my neck. It was freezing outside, but in here, my heavy coat made me hot.

I swung my legs as Tyson and I waited.

By the stage, Aunt Billie was talking to a man.

Her friend Kyle wiped down a table near us.

It was Saturday, and Mom and Dad were working at the hospital. Aunt Billie had been watching us at Center Stage Café. She sings here every week.

"Who's Aunt Billie talking to?" I asked Kyle.

He moved onto the next table. "That's Mr. Novak. He's the new manager."

I blinked. "Aunt Billie has a new boss?"

Grinning, he said, "Nope. Your aunt got a promotion. She and Mr. Novak are co-managers."

"What does that mean?" I asked.

"They're both the boss."

"Oh." No wonder Aunt Billie seemed busy lately.

Kyle jerked his head at the board. "Did you see that flier?"

Aunt Billie was still talking. I shrugged off my coat and stood to read the flier.

At the top, it said: "The Matchmaker." Below that, I read: "Meet your match this Valentine's Day! Judges will pair up bands ahead of time. At the event, you only have to beat your match to win! All winners will get tickets to a surprise event."

Lines for sign-ups filled the rest of the paper. Most of them were already full.

The Major Eights could perform at the café! I couldn't wait to tell Maggie, Jasmine, and Becca. We had to get to work on some new material. Valentine's Day was only one week away!

I spun around and bumped right into someone.

It was a girl. She was taller than me. Straight, brown hair fell past her shoulders. Two other girls stood behind her.

"Hey, watch it!" the girl snapped.

I blinked. "Um, sorry."

"*Excuse* me." She tapped her foot, waiting for me to move.

Confused, I stepped back.

"Here it is," she said to the other girls. She pointed at the flier. Taking out a pen, she wrote: "Cassie and the Cools."

"Are you guys in a band?" I asked.

"I'm Cassie." The tall girl said, tossing her hair. "These are my backup singers, Izzy and Cleo."

"So, you're a singer?" I asked. "Me too!"

"Really?" She faked a yawn. "My sister Cleo and I just moved here. Our dad's the new manager of this place."

"Oh," I said. "You mean, co-manager. With my Aunt Billie."

She acted like she hadn't heard me. "In our old town, I won lots of singing awards. We're so going to clean up at the Matchmaker." She and Izzy high-fived.

"Well, okay. I guess our band will see you there."

As Cassie and her 'Cools' left, I tugged my coat back on.

Why had Cassie been so rude?

Journey to some magical places, rock out, and find your inner superhero with these other chapter book series from **Little Bee Books**!

little bee books
an imprint of Bonnier Publishing USA